Martin by Himself

Gloria Skurzynski

Illustrated by Lynn Munsinger

Houghton Mifflin Company 1979

Library of Congress Cataloging in Publication Data

Skurzynski, Gloria.
  Martin by himself.

    SUMMARY: Martin doesn't like coming home to an empty
house when his mother goes back to work.
    [1. Mothers–Employment–Fiction] I. Munsinger,
Lynn. II. Title.
PZ7.S6287Mar   [E]   79-11748

ISBN 0-395-28271-3

For Lauren

It was raining hard when Martin got out of school. While he was pulling his hat down over his ears, he stepped in a puddle.

Martin looked at his feet. They were wet and muddy.

"Oh well," he said to himself, "my shoes are already muddy. It won't hurt if I walk through some more puddles." So he splashed through oozy mud all the way home.

When he reached his back door, he looked at his shoes again. They were so caked with mud that the shoelaces stuck out like cats' whiskers.

"Mother," he called loudly, so she could hear him through the door. "Mother, my shoes are dirty."

Martin waited for his mother to come out and help him take off his muddy shoes, but she didn't come.

Then Martin remembered. His mother wasn't home today. She had gone to work at the hospital. This was her first day at work. The house was empty.

Martin reached inside his jacket, where he could feel the brand-new house key his mother had given him. The key was hanging on a shiny chain, and the chain was pinned inside his jacket. He took out the key and unlocked the back door.

Inside, the house seemed very strange. It was so quiet that Martin could hear the clock ticking and the refrigerator humming. He put his books down on the kitchen table. Then he looked at the floor. There was a line of muddy footprints on it.

Mother wouldn't like that.

But Mother wasn't home.

On the kitchen table was a plate with two cookies, and beside the plate was a note. It said, "Martin, here's a snack for you. I'll be home at five o'clock. Love, Mother."

Martin looked at the clock. It was four o'clock.

He touched the cookies and made little half-circles in the chocolate chips with his fingernail. But he didn't eat the cookies. He didn't want them. He pushed the plate away.

He took off his wet hat and his wet jacket and dropped
them on the floor. He stepped out of his wet pants and left
them on the floor. When he looked at his messy clothes lying
there all soggy and limp, he started to shiver.

Martin went to his bedroom closet and poked through it, pulling things off hangers. He looked for something that would feel soft and warm and dry. He decided to put on his pajama pants. Mother wouldn't want him to wear his pajama pants in the middle of the afternoon. But Mother wasn't home.

Martin got a funny feeling in his insides. He thought maybe he might be hungry after all, so he went back to the kitchen. Martin still didn't want the cookies Mother had left for him, but a peanut butter and banana sandwich sounded good. He piled peanut butter thick on a slice of bread, and put a whole banana on top of it.

While he was putting away the jar, he got a blob of peanut butter on the refrigerator door. The peanut butter blob almost made a picture. It looked like a car.

Martin opened the jar again, stuck in his finger, and dug out a fat swirl of peanut butter. He made another car on the refrigerator door with peanut butter. Then he made a man. Then an airplane. Then a house.

By the time he finished his peanut butter pictures, the jar was empty. Martin knew that Mother wouldn't like peanut butter all over the refrigerator. But Mother wasn't home.

He licked his fingers and looked at the clock. The clock said 4:15.

"Four-fifteen!" Martin said out loud. "It must be later than that. Maybe the clock is broken." He went to the telephone, looked at the list of Numbers Frequently Called, and dialed Time of Day.

"Save your money at City Bank," the telephone voice said. "The time is fifteen minutes after four."

"I thought it must be later than that," Martin said to the voice. "I'm home all by myself."

"Save your money at City Bank," the telephone voice said. "The time is fifteen minutes after four."

"I thought maybe our clock was broken," Martin told the voice. "It seems like a long time since I came home."

"Save your money at City Bank," the voice said again. "The time is sixteen minutes after four."

"I thought it must be close to five o'clock," Martin said. "That's when Mother will come home from . . ."

"Save your . . ."

Martin hung up the phone.

He didn't know what to do with himself. His mother had told him to do his homework when he came home from school, but he didn't feel like doing homework. He didn't feel like playing with his cars, either. And he couldn't play checkers by himself, could he?

He looked out the window. It was still raining outside. The dog next door, Gus, was standing inside his fenced-in pen, looking droopy and forlorn. Gus was wet and muddy, just the way Martin had been.

"Gus looks so sad," Martin said to himself. "He doesn't have anyone to play with. Poor dog, I bet he's lonesome. He's all by himself. Poor, poor dog, maybe I ought to bring him over here to my house, so he won't be all alone. Mother wouldn't like me to bring Gus in here. But Mother isn't home."

Martin ran through the raindrops to the yard next door and unlatched the gate to Gus's pen.

For a few seconds the dog just looked at him as though he were wondering what Martin wanted him to do. Then Gus leaped through the gate and started to run in circles on the wet grass.

"Hey Gus! Here, boy, come into my house," Martin called. Finally he caught Gus by the collar and dragged him through the back door. "There, isn't that better?" Martin asked him. "Now you won't have to be all alone anymore."

Gus shook himself hard. Drops of water and mud flew all over the place — on the floor, on the table, the chairs, and the walls. Mother wasn't going to like mud splattered all over her kitchen. But Mother wasn't home.

Gus started to sniff. He sniffed just like a cartoon dog, with his nose on the floor and his long ears hanging. His feet seemed to move by themselves. He walked down the hall with his nose against the carpet, sniffing all the while. Martin followed him.

Suddenly the telephone rang, loud and shrill. "Maybe it's Mother calling me," Martin shouted, running to answer it. But it was a wrong number.

Then Martin heard a crash so loud it made him jump all over. He ran to the living room. Gus stood there wagging his big hairy tail. He was grinning and his tongue was hanging out of the side of his mouth. He had knocked over a big flower pot that held Mother's favorite plant.

Mother really loved that plant. She loved it so much that she gave it a name — Julia. Julia was lying flat on the floor with her roots bare naked. There was dirt from the flower pot all over the place.

"Gus, you dumb dog, why did you do that?" Martin screeched. He went to the kitchen for a spoon, then got down on his knees to scoop the dirt back into the pot. While he was spooning dirt, he looked up to see what Gus was doing.

Gus was standing next to the coffee table. The dog's back leg was in the air, and he was . . . OH NO!

"Gus, STOP IT!" Martin screamed. "You're making a puddle all over the carpet. STOP IT!"

Gus looked at Martin, but he kept right on doing what he was doing, and Martin didn't know how to stop him. Martin just stood there, clenching his fists and biting his lip. Mother *really* wasn't going to like that. Not at all. Not one little bit!

Martin ran to the bathroom and got two towels off the
rack. He knew they were Mother's best towels, but he didn't
have time to hunt for old ones. He took them to the living
room and tried to wipe up the big wet spot on the carpet.

The carpet stayed wet, but the towels got wet, too. And
they smelled bad.

Martin ran back to the bathroom and threw the towels into the bathtub. He poured in some of Mother's bubble bath to take the smell out of the towels, then turned on the water, hard. He put in more bubble bath, and more, because he could still smell the smell.

While the tub was filling up, Martin thought, "I'd better see what Gus is doing."

Gus was licking peanut butter off the refrigerator.

"You better get out of here, you dumb dog, before you get in more trouble," Martin shouted. "Go on, Gus, go home!"

Gus just looked at him.

"Please, Gus!"

Gus wagged his tail and grinned.

"GUS, SCRAM!"

Gus scratched his ear with his hind leg.

"The water!" Martin yelled. "I forgot to turn off the water in the tub!"

In the bathroom, bubbles rose high in the tub, piling up in mounds like soft whipped cream. They slid smoothly over the side of the tub and soaked into the bathroom rug, popping with quiet little pops. Martin turned off the water and ran back to the kitchen.

Bubble Bath

"I've got to get you out of here," he hollered at Gus.
"You've already got me into so much trouble . . . Wait, maybe
this will work!"

Martin took a piece of meatloaf out of the refrigerator and
took a step toward the door. "See, nice meat. Come and get
it, Gus."

Gus moved about two inches closer to Martin and gobbled
down the meat.

Martin took the whole plate of meatloaf out of the refrigerator and fed it to Gus, one slice at a time, as he coaxed the
dog toward the door. By the time Gus was outside and the
door was shut behind him, all the meatloaf was gone.

"Whew," Martin sighed. Then he looked around him.

The house was a mess.

Martin's muddy footprints covered the kitchen floor.

His wet clothes lay where he had dropped them.

Muddy splatters from Gus were all over the kitchen.

The refrigerator door was smeared with peanut butter.

The bathroom was full of bubbles.

The living room carpet was covered with dirt.

Julia was probably dead.

And worst of all, there was a smelly wet spot on the carpet.

Mother isn't going to like this, Martin thought. In fact, she's going to HATE it! "But Mother isn't home," he said out loud.

Martin felt awful. He felt as though he had a big, empty hole inside him. Then he started to get angry. "Why aren't you home, Mother?" he shouted to the empty house. "These things don't happen when you're here!"

He looked at the clock. It was 4:45. Maybe he'd have time to clean up before Mother got home, if he could only figure out where to begin. He picked up his muddy shoes, but he didn't know where to put them.

While Martin was standing with his shoes in his hand, he heard a key turning in the front door lock. Then the door opened and his mother's voice called out, "Martin, I'm home."

"You're early," Martin answered.

"I thought I'd better come home a little early because I didn't want to leave you alone too long on my first day away," his mother's voice said.

Martin heard his mother go into the living room. He heard her voice, all choked up, say, "Julia!" and then he didn't hear anything at all. Nothing.

After a long time, he heard his mother walk to the bathroom. She looked inside. Then she came into the kitchen. She looked at Martin.

"*Why?*" she asked.

"You weren't home when I came home from school," Martin said. Tears came into his eyes.

"But you knew I wouldn't be home," his mother answered. "You knew I would be working in the hospital."

"I was all by myself," Martin said. "I didn't like it."

"All by yourself? How could you make so much mess all by yourself in forty-five minutes?"

"I didn't have anything else to do," Martin said.

His mother made a small sound that might have been a giggle. Then she sighed, a sigh that seemed to come from deep inside her. She sat down and took Martin's hand.

"Martin, you know I have to go to work," she said. "The hospital needs me. The sick people in the hospital need me."

"I need you too, Mother," Martin said.

"And I need you, Martin." She touched his cheek softly with her hand. "I thought you were old enough to stay by yourself for an hour after school each day, but I guess I was wrong. I'll get a baby-sitter to keep you company."

Martin stood up straight. "I'm not a baby," he said, "and I don't need a sitter. Give me another chance. I know I did everything wrong today, but it won't happen again. I can take care of myself. You'll see."

"You just told me you didn't have anything to do after school."

"I'll find something to do," Martin promised. "Tomorrow I'll wipe the bubbles out of the bathroom. The next day I'll

clean the peanut butter off the refrigerator. The next day I'll clean the dirt off the living-room carpet."

"Those things can't wait," Mother said. "We'll have to do them tonight."

Martin thought hard. "Mother, I figured it out," he said. "When I come home from school, I'll change my clothes and have a snack. Then I'll go outside and take Gus for a walk. Poor old Gus, he stays in his back yard all day long and he's lonely. He'd like me to take him for nice long walks — outside, where he can't get into any trouble."

"That's a good idea," Mother said. "I'm certain Gus's owners would like that."

"That way you can help the sick people in the hospital, and I'll be helping Gus," Martin said. Suddenly he felt better. The house would still seem strange and empty when he came home from school, but he'd have something important to keep him busy until his mother got back.

"Since we're both going to be helpers," Mother said, "let's help each other. We'll clean up this mess right now, and then we'll get out the meatloaf and fix a nice dinner for the two of us."

"Um . . . uh . . . ," Martin said, "why don't we cook hot dogs instead? I'll help."